JUV
QL
767
.P68
1990

Powzyk, Joyce Ann.

Animal camouflage

ANIMAL CAMOUFLAGE

· *A Closer Look* ·

by Joyce Powzyk

Bradbury Press   New York

While researching animal camouflage, I found that there are many different, and sometimes conflicting, classifications of camouflage types. This book presents general classifications of animal camouflage and serves as an introduction to this complex subject.

I would like to thank Mary La Croy at the American Museum of Natural History, New York, for her assistance in obtaining the necessary bird specimens. I also wish to thank my editor, Barbara Lalicki, and designer, Julie Quan, who guided me to completion on this project. And, finally, my warmest appreciation to SHD.

Bradbury Press
An Affiliate of Macmillan, Inc.
866 Third Avenue, New York, NY 10022
Collier Macmillan Canada, Inc.

Printed and bound in the United States of America
First Edition
10 9 8 7 6 5 4 3 2 1

The text of this book is set in 14 point Fairfield Medium.
The illustrations are rendered in watercolor and colored pencil.
Typography by Julie Quan

LIBRARY OF CONGRESS CATALOGING-IN-PUBLICATION DATA
Powzyk, Joyce Ann.
Animal camouflage: a closer look.
Includes index.
Summary: Introduces general ways animals camouflage themselves, such as coloration, mimicry, and disguise, and discusses how specific animals protect themselves using these techniques.
1. Camouflage (Biology)—Juvenile Literature.
[1. Camouflage (Biology)] I. Title.
QL767.P68   1990   591.57'2   89-9848
ISBN 0-02-774980-0

For my family

CONTENTS

What is animal camouflage?

Camouflage is the use of color, pattern, and/or shape to hide an animal's presence. Animals that are camouflaged have security in their environment. Their camouflage helps them to go unnoticed as they search for food or a mate.

Animals that are hunted as prey often use camouflage to hide from predators. Yet predators also use camouflage as they stalk and hunt. Some animals combine different types of camouflage, which usually increases their ability to conceal themselves. Others add to their camouflage by moving in a certain way for long periods of time, or by not moving at all. It should be remembered, however, that camouflage does not protect against those predators that hunt using their senses of touch, smell, or hearing.

This book includes examples of camouflage from around the world. Although each creature has a specific way of camouflaging itself, you'll begin to see that the basic techniques are the same. Once you become familiar with them, take a trip outside. Look for an insect or a bird or other animal that may be using camouflage to hide. If you look closely, there are many to be found, no matter where you live.

Types of camouflage featured in this book

CONCEALING COLORATION

> Body colors that match or blend with an animal's immediate surroundings.

DISRUPTIVE COLORATION

> Stripes, spots, or other bold color patterns that disrupt—or break up—the visible outline of an animal's body, making the animal's shape hard to see.

DISGUISE

> Looking like a specific *object*, such as a leaf, twig, or stone.

MIMICRY

> Looking like another *animal,* and often behaving like that animal.

And the more unusual forms of camouflage:

MASKING

> When an animal gathers materials from the surrounding environment to construct a concealing mask.

CONCEALMENT OF THE EYE

> A stripe, pattern, or covering that makes an animal's eye hard to recognize.

Parson's Chameleon

A Parson's chameleon clutches the branch of an ylang-ylang (e-lang-e-lang) tree as it slowly prowls through the vegetation. The lizard's skin is a rich shade of green that blends perfectly with the greens of the tree's leaves. It moves its body in short rocking motions, in a way that resembles the swaying of windblown leaves and branches.

The chameleon is hungry. Its eyes scan the leaves, each rotating independently of the other as they search for prey. When a large fly lands on a nearby leaf, the chameleon intently focuses on the insect. Its body stretches out, slowly, to get within striking range. Suddenly the lizard's long tongue shoots out. The fly is gummed up and quickly swallowed.

The chameleon is a champion at camouflage. It can change its skin color from green to dark brown to orange and to many colors in-between. The skin of the lizard is made up of four layers. Each layer can produce different colors. When several layers combine their colors, the lizard can match a variety of backgrounds.

To blend with the tree's green leaves, the chameleon exhibits a yellow color caused by a pigment, and a blue caused by structures in its skin: Yellow and blue together make the color green. For a darker green color, the chameleon also exhibits large amounts of the black pigment melanin.

If moved to a brown setting, the chameleon changes its coloration by exhibiting orange and black pigments: Orange and black together make the color brown.

Kirk's Dik-dik

A pride of lions walks by the thornbushes that grow beneath a large fever tree. The lions pause in the tree's shade, panting heavily. Moments later, they move out, and continue toward a herd of antelopes in the hazy distance.

After the cats have passed, a Kirk's dik-dik breaks from its statuelike stance and takes a few cautious steps, moving one leg at a time. It had been standing no more than thirty feet from where the lions rested. The tiny dik-dik was lucky that it was downwind and the lions did not smell it. But they also failed to see the tiny antelope. Though it was terrified, the dik-dik remained completely motionless, so that its brown coloration blended with the brown landscape.

Small antelopes are extremely vulnerable and often rely on their fur color as camouflage. For this reason the dik-dik is usually found near shrubs or tall grass, which help to conceal its presence.

A baby dik-dik adds to its camouflage by flattening its body close to the ground. Its brown form looks like nothing more than a hump of dirt and grass. Because a newborn lacks a scent, it often goes undetected.

Livingstone's Turaco

In the dense African rain forest, a Livingstone's turaco searches for ripe fruit as it jumps from branch to branch. The trees are covered with vines and ferns, all competing for the sun's rays. The green bird suddenly spies another turaco in a neighboring tree and moves through the branches to investigate.

The two birds quickly recognize each other as prospective mates and begin an elaborate display of feathers. One turaco shakes its head and extends its wings in courtship. This exposes its bright crimson flight feathers. The other turaco watches intently and then flashes its wings in response.

Most birds are capable of seeing red, yellow, and green colors. Therefore the turaco's red flight feathers and eye markings are important signals that help these birds communicate. But once a turaco stops its wing flashing, the bird's green body blends into the foliage so that hawks and other predators can't spot it.

The turaco has struck an important balance. It has green feathers for camouflage and bright crimson feathers for display during courtship.

The bright crimson color on the turaco's flight feathers is produced by the pigment turacin, which contains copper and is found in no other animal.

Ermine and Snowshoe Hare

The ermine eagerly follows the fresh scent of a hare through the newly fallen snow. Suddenly it stops, for it has seen movement up ahead. A white snowshoe hare lifts its head and surveys the winter landscape while chewing on a willow stem. Failing to see or smell the intruder, the hare continues to feed. Unable to contain itself any longer, the ermine charges, but the powdery snow slows its attack. The hare recognizes its foe and panics. With a kick from its oversized hind legs, it jumps high into the air and swiftly outruns its short-legged pursuer.

The ermine and hare both have white fur to conceal themselves in the bleak winter landscape. But when spring arrives, a change is triggered by the increased hours of daylight. Both animals gradually shed their white fur for brown fur, to better blend with the grass and leaf litter.

The brown color of the summer coat arises from the pigment melanin, which is manufactured by the body during the digestion of food.

The white color of the winter fur is caused by tiny bubble-shaped structures inside each hair, which reflect all light. The hare's spring coat still shows some white fur.

Satyr Tragopan

A female satyr tragopan (say-ter trag-e-pan) sits on her jumbled nest of twigs and branches high above the ground in a tall evergreen tree. Her body is flattened to conceal her presence while she keeps the two eggs buried in her breast feathers warm.

From a nearby perch her mate booms out a challenge call of "wah, waah, oo-ah," telling other males that this is his territory. The male tragopan is brilliantly colored, with a deep red breast splattered with spots of white. He glides to the ground and begins to search for insects and plant shoots. Suddenly the tragopan is startled by the rustling of leaves. A fox is creeping through the brush, trying to get closer to the feeding bird. With a whir of its wings, the tragopan rises into the air and disappears into the forest, leaving no hint that his mate is close by.

The female tragopan is not as brilliantly colored as her mate. Her coloration is made up of different shades of brown. This concealing coloration provides security for the mother, who has the greater role in raising the hatchlings into adulthood. Her brown colors serve as camouflage while she incubates the eggs, and later when she leads the baby birds through the forest in search of food.

The male tragopan uses his song and flashy colors to attract a mate.

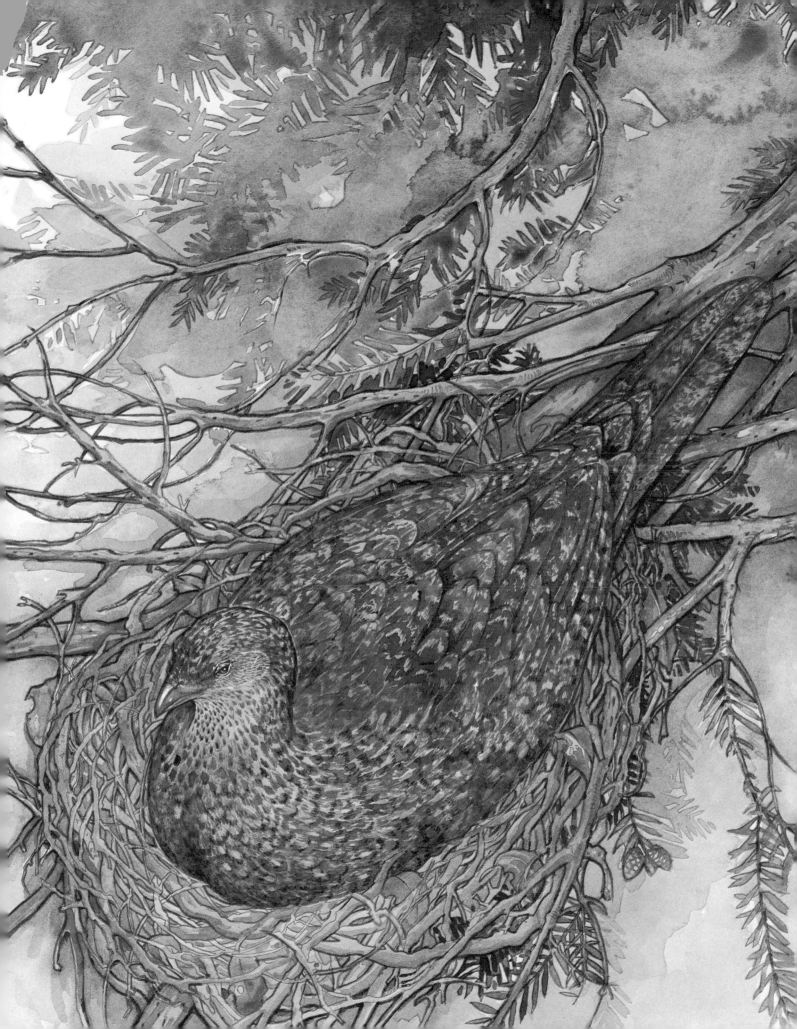

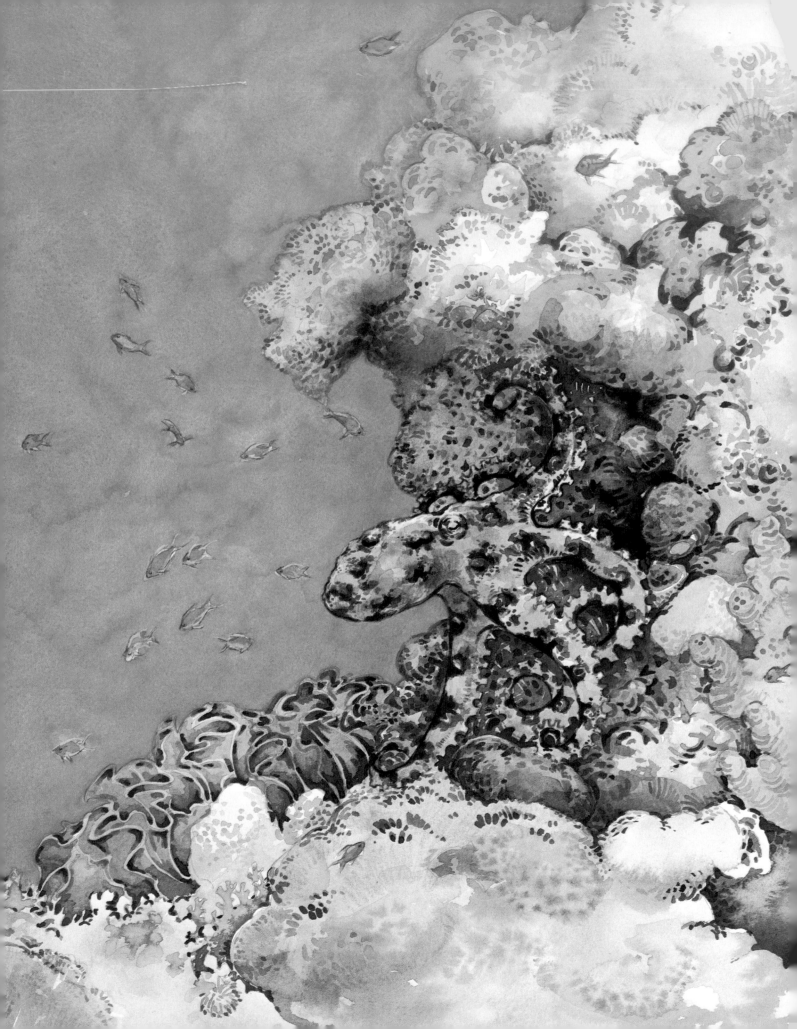

Blue-ringed Octopus

Lurking in a hollow of a large coral reef, a hungry blue-ringed octopus waits. A crab ambles by and the octopus stretches out a long suckered arm and gathers it in. The struggling crab is given a sharp bite from the octopus's parrotlike beak. A poison carried in the octopus's saliva takes effect, and the crab goes limp. The octopus begins to devour its prize as it settles back into the sheltering reef.

The octopus's coloration is very similar to the colors of the surrounding coral. This is concealing coloration. But there is another form of camouflage at work here. The large blotches on its skin help to disrupt the octopus's form and it is difficult to see where the octopus ends and the reef begins. Disruptive coloration increases the likelihood that this animal will not be seen.

When an octopus moves about its underwater realm, it must change its skin color to match new backgrounds. A blue-green octopus can transform itself into a mottled purple-brown octopus within seconds. No other animal can change color faster, except the octopus's close relatives: the squid and the cuttlefish.

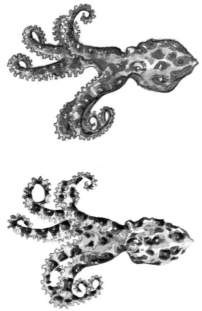

When the octopus is threatened, the camouflage can turn into a warning coloration. The animal's colors intensify, almost reaching a jewel-like quality, signaling others that the octopus has a deadly poisonous bite.

Spotted Leopard

Out on the African plain, a large spotted leopard maneuvers through the tangled branches of a towering acacia (a-kay-she-a) tree. Suddenly it freezes. The leopard has sighted prey. It intently watches a small herd of gazelles as they meander toward the tree, grazing. The gazelles do not see the motionless predator on its lofty perch.

When the leopard is still, its black spots break up or disrupt its shape and the cat blends into the maze of sun-dappled vegetation. However, when the leopard moves, this disruptive camouflage stops working. That is why the leopard stays perfectly still until the last possible moment, when it charges its prey, often leaving no time for escape.

There is a black leopard, or panther, that is the same species as the spotted leopard. Its black fur is caused by an overabundance of the pigment melanin. Still present are the spots, which can be seen on the animal's coat when viewed in direct light. The melanistic leopard usually lives in the jungle, where its dark coat helps it blend into the shadows of the lush foliage.

African Flower Mantis

In a cluster of pink petals on a rosebay bush, an African flower mantis sits, poised and ready to strike. As a breeze blows the soft petals, the mantis slowly rocks back and forth, pretending to be ruffled by the wind. A sphinx moth comes to the rosebay bush and begins to probe the blossoms for nectar with its long tongue. The moth moves from one flower to the next, until it comes to the blossom on which the mantis sits. Swiftly, the mantis strikes. It grabs the moth with its oversized front legs, and immediately pulls the victim toward its mouth as it starts to feed.

Pigments that are made by the mantis as it digests its food give the insect its pink and green coloration. Disguised as part of the plant's blossoms, the mantis can sit openly on a rosebay bush yet blend in at the same time. Those insects that feed on flower nectar often fail to notice the waiting flower mantis. They are caught unexpectedly in a death grasp by this small yet powerful hunter.

If threatened by a bird, the mantis can change its disguise to scare off an intruder. The camouflaging colors quickly turn into warning colors when the mantis takes an aggressive posture with its body and legs to display a set of false "eyes." Birds are put off by this and flee from the display.

Venezuelan Katydid

As the sun begins to set, a male Venezuelan katydid begins a loud, rasping melody by rubbing its wings together. His mating song floats out over the woodlands to lure a female to his location. When it hears an unusual noise, the katydid falls silent. The insect does not want to draw a predator to its hideout. Later, when the woods are again peaceful, the katydid resumes its rhythmic song.

The Venezuelan katydid is a type of long-horned grasshopper. But this species is unlike most because it has hard spikes on its legs and body. Its shape and light green color closely resemble the surrounding moss or bark. With such an effective disguise, the katydid is almost invisible as it sits on a moss-covered branch. Despite the insect's relatively large size, a hungry bird would have a difficult time finding it.

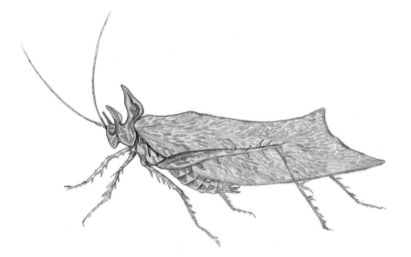

The front wings of the Venezuelan katydid camouflage the insect by resembling vegetation. The base of these wings, rubbed together, make the katydid's song.

Batfish

Several young batfish swim between the submerged roots of a mangrove tree, their bodies gently swaying with the river's current. A kingfisher hovers overhead. It spies the fish and dives into the river to catch one, but misses.

The batfish are startled. They swim down toward the river's bottom and lie on their sides close to the dead yellow-brown mangrove leaves. The kingfisher, confused since it can no longer recognize the fish from the leaf litter, flies off. The batfish move slowly along the river's bottom, propelled with the help of their strong side fins. Eventually, they relax. The fish begin to swim upright, away from the bottom.

The young batfish have a remarkable body shape. They look like mangrove leaves. This unique disguise, together with the uncommon behavior of swimming on their sides, lets them hide in the mangrove leaves that have settled on the river's bottom.

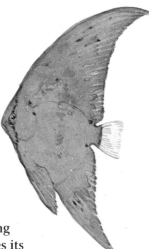

Most fish have a noticeable tail fin but the young batfish's tail fin is transparent, which enhances its disguising mangrove leaf shape.

Hover Fly

A hover fly moves around a flowering bush, landing occasionally to probe the flowers with its tongue in search of sweet nectar. It is joined by a bumblebee, which also hovers near the bush, buzzing loudly. The bee has a powerful stinger to use against any bird, fox, or other animal that tries to eat it.

Flies do not have stingers. Yet this hover fly has protection.

With a yellow-and-black abdomen, the hover fly mimics the appearance of the bumblebee. It also creates a loud buzzing noise with its wings. Any predator that has experienced a painful sting will avoid bumblebees—and those hover flies that mimic bees.

Viceroy Butterfly

Butterflies flutter over a large field of red clover. Two look remarkably alike. Both have striking orange-and-black markings. One is a monarch, a large butterfly which glides majestically along, fluttering in short bursts. The other, a viceroy, is smaller.

The monarch's bright colors serve as a warning to birds, for if caught, this butterfly cannot be eaten. In its body are poisons that cause the monarch to have a strong, bitter taste. Any bird that has tried to eat a monarch will remember the bad taste along with the bold markings and will avoid these butterflies.

The viceroy mimics the monarch. Even though this butterfly is good to eat, birds that have sampled a monarch will also shy away from the viceroy.

Kelp Crab

A small crab is nestled in the roots of a giant kelp plant, slowly munching on a piece of shellfish. Covering its back are strips of green seaweed which act as a cloak, hiding the crab.

The kelp crab was not born with camouflage, but has created its own. It has constructed a "mask" of seaweed which keeps it hidden.

The crab creates the mask by grabbing a piece of kelp with one of its clawed arms. The kelp is brought to its mouth and chewed. The roughened seaweed tip is then rubbed against the top of the crab's shell. Small curved bristles on the shell snag the seaweed and hold it in place. This is repeated many times, until the shell is covered. With its mask in place, the kelp crab is safe from hungry sea otters that also comb the twisted kelp beds in search of food.

As it grows, a kelp crab sheds its old shell and replaces it with a new, larger shell. Since the old masking materials are also discarded, the kelp crab quickly gathers new seaweed and within hours is again fully camouflaged.

Leaf-tailed Gecko

Gripping the bark with its clawed feet, a leaf-tailed gecko clings to the trunk of a eucalyptus tree with its head pointing toward the ground. Several ants pass within reach, and the gecko's tongue darts out to nab one after the other.

Though the lizard is not hiding, it is invisible to any predator that relies on its sight to hunt. The gecko's skin matches the colors of the tree bark to which it clings. Adding to this concealing coloration is the gecko's tail, which, with its flat shape, is disguised as a dead leaf. By hugging the tree, the lizard fails to cast a shadow, which again reduces its chances of being seen. But the most unusual camouflage is the gecko's eyes. The iris is brown, the same speckled brown as the lizard's skin, and each pupil is a thin vertical slit. Predators that search for prey by looking for a set of round eyes are fooled by the gecko.

Concealment of the eye is an uncommon form of camouflage and is used by few creatures. By using several different types of camouflage, the gecko increases its chances of survival.

The gecko does not have the round, dark pupils most predators are searching for.

OTHER EXAMPLES OF CAMOUFLAGED ANIMALS

young crocodile
(concealment of the eye)

clearwing moth imitating
a hornet (mimicry)

a true hornet

caddis fly larva with body
case made of sticks
(masking)

caddis fly larva
without body case

leafy sea dragon in
seaweed (disguise)

leafy sea dragon

willow ptarmigan in snowy
landscape (concealing coloration)

willow ptarmigan

Oriental leaf butterfly at rest
(disguise)

Oriental leaf
butterfly in flight

leopard frog in grass
(disruptive coloration)

leopard frog

harmless milk snake
imitating a poisonous
coral snake (mimicry)

poisonous coral snake

GLOSSARY

ACACIA TREE: A member of the *Mimosa* family, this tree is native to warmer regions of the world such as Australia and Africa. All of the varieties have small green leaves and many are also equipped with sharp spines.

COLOR: Color is determined primarily by the nature of the light that is reflected from a surface (hair, skin, feathers, etc.) either by pigments, structures, or a combination of the two.
- pigmented color: Color caused by pigments which are either ingested or manufactured in the body from digestion of the animal's food.
- structural color: Color caused by the structure of a surface, such as minute ridges or scales.

FEVER TREE: A common name used to describe a type of acacia tree that often grows along the rivers and streams of Africa.

IRIS: The colored portion of the eye.

KELP: A type of green seaweed with long leaves and stalks that grows in large beds along the coastline from California to Alaska and along parts of the Asian coastline.

KINGFISHER: A bird often found near water that preys upon fish, insects, and other aquatic organisms by diving down into the water and seizing its victim in a strong beak.

MANGROVE TREE: A tree that grows in dense thickets and sends out numerous prop roots to support itself above the brackish (somewhat salty) coastal waters of the tropics.

MELANIN: A common pigment found in animals that produces black, brown, and occasionally yellow or red colors. A melanistic animal is completely black, due to an overabundance of the melanin pigment.

PIGMENT: A general term for a chemical substance that produces color, including some shades of black and white.

PUPIL: The dark center of an eye that takes in light. The pupil usually appears round or elliptical.

TURACIN: A pigment that is partially composed of copper and produces a deep red or crimson color. This pigment is named after the only animals in which it is found, the turacos.

YLANG-YLANG TREE: A tree that is a member of the custard-apple family native to the Philippines and adjacent areas. Its fragrant yellow flower is distilled and used as a perfume base.

SUGGESTIONS FOR FURTHER READING

Owen, Denis. *Camouflage and Mimicry.* Chicago: The University of Chicago Press, 1980.

Oxford Scientific Film. *Hide and Seek.* Edited by Jennifer Coldrey and Karen Goldie-Morrison. New York: G. P. Putnam's Sons, 1986.

Patent, Dorothy H. *Animal and Plant Mimicry.* New York: Holiday House, 1978.

Simon, Hilda. *Chameleons and Other Quick-Change Artists.* New York: Dodd, Mead & Company, 1973.

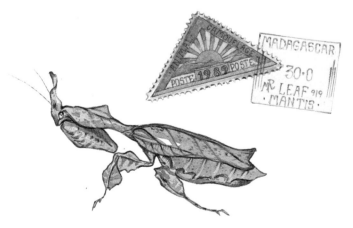

ADDITIONAL INFORMATION ON THE FEATURED ANIMALS

Name	Latin	Distribution
Parson's Chameleon (*Chamaeleo parsonii*)		Madagascar
Kirk's Dik-dik (*Rhynchotragus kirki*)		Africa
Livingstone's Turaco (*Tauraco persa livingstonii*)		East Africa
Ermine (*Mustela erminea*)		North America, Europe & Asia
Snowshoe Hare (*Lepus americanus*)		Canada
Satyr Tragopan (*Tragopan satyra*)		Central & Eastern Himalaya Mountains
Blue-ringed Octopus (*Hapalochlaena maculosa*)		Coastal Waters of Eastern Australia, north to Indonesia & the Philippines
Spotted Leopard (*Panthera pardus*)		Africa
African Flower Mantis (*Pseudocreobotra wahlbergi*)		Africa
Venezuelan Katydid (*Markia hystrix*)		South America
Batfish (*Platax orbicularis*)		Coastal waters of the Indo-Pacific
Hover Fly (*Merodon clavipes*)		Africa
Viceroy Butterfly (*Limenitis archippus*)		North America & the West Indies
Kelp Crab (*Pugettia dalli*)		Coastal waters of California
Leaf-tailed Gecko (*Phyllurus cornutus*)		Northeastern Australia

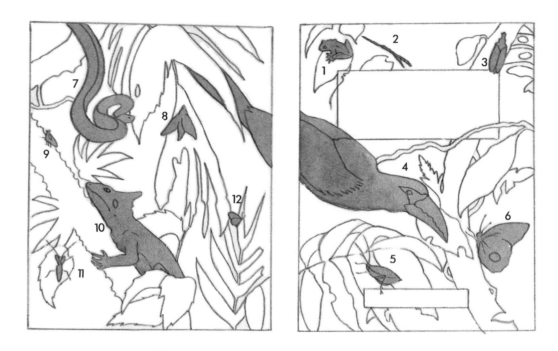

The animals pictured on the cover can be found in Central and South America. They are:

1. Phyllomedusa tree frog
2. Stick insect
3. Lantern fly
4. Emerald toucanet
5. Green-leaf katydid
6. Owl butterfly

7. Parrot snake
8. Green sphinx moth
9. Horned treehopper
10. Basilisk lizard
11. Praying mantis
12. Glass-winged butterfly

The title page illustration shows South American leaf katydids; a Malagasy leaf mantis is seen on page 37; and green and yellow tree hoppers decorate page 2.

INDEX